DAVID McPHAIL

The Searcher and Old Tree

Charlesbridge

To my collaborators,

Susan and Yolanda

2011 First paperback edition
Copyright © 2008 by David McPhail
All rights reserved, including the right of reproduction in whole
or in part in any form. Charlesbridge and colophon are
registered trademarks of Charlesbridge Publishing, Inc.

Published by Charlesbridge
85 Main Street
Watertown, MA 02472
(617) 926-0329
www.charlesbridge.com

Library of Congress Cataloging-in-Publication Data
McPhail, David, 1940–
    The Searcher and Old Tree / David McPhail.
        p. cm.
    Summary: A raccoon forages for food at night and at dawn
returns to its home in a strong, old tree, which safely shelters
the raccoon through wild winds and ferocious rain so that it can
go out searching for food again.
    ISBN 978-1-58089-223-0 (reinforced for library use)
    ISBN 978-1-58089-224-7 (softcover)
[1. Raccoons—Fiction. 2. Trees—Fiction. 3. Storms—Fiction.]
I. Title.
PZ7.M2427Se 2008
[E]—dc22   2007008114

Printed in China
(hc) 10 9 8 7 6 5 4 3 2
(sc) 10 9 8 7 6 5 4 3 2 1

Illustrations done in pen and ink and watercolor on illustration board
Display type and text type set in Weiss
Color separations by Chroma Graphics, Singapore
Manufactured by Regent Publishing Services, Hong Kong
Printed September 2010 in Shenzhen, Guangdong, China
Production supervision by Brian G. Walker
Designed by Susan Mallory Sherman

After a long night's search for food,
the Searcher heads home.

It has been a fruitful trip, and his belly is full.

Dawn is near—and so is home.

It is time for the Searcher to sleep.

He climbs up Old Tree's sturdy trunk.

He follows his tail around in circles and collapses
in a heap on Old Tree's familiar branches.

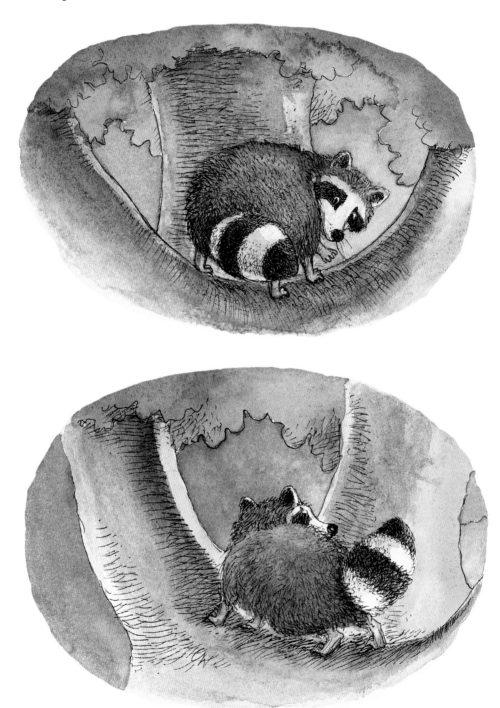

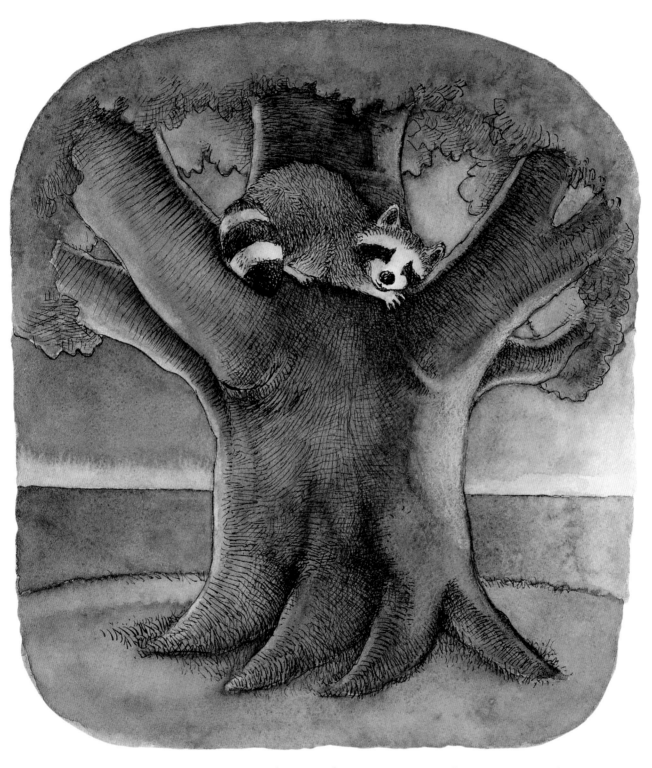

He closes his eyes and goes to sleep.

While the Searcher sleeps, the wind starts to blow.

It whips the waves.

The wind blows harder. The waves slam against the shore.

BOOM! The ground shakes.

The wind rips through Old Tree's branches.

The waves continue to pound, surge, and crash.

SMASH! The Searcher sleeps on.

The wind is howling
furiously now. Old
Tree is bent nearly to
the ground. The waves
rise and curl.

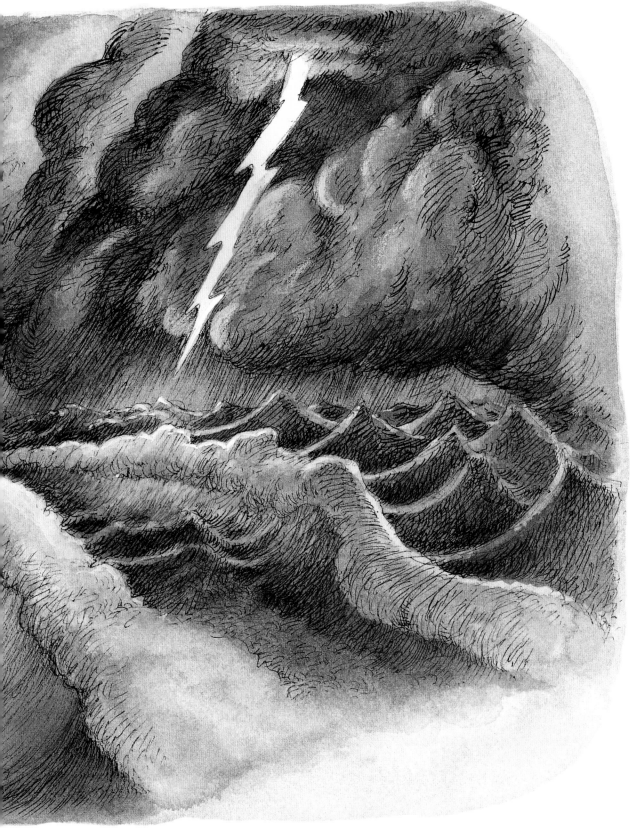

The wind and waves increase in ferocity throughout the day.

The wind tries to pull
Old Tree out by the roots.

It can't.

The wind shrieks. The waves explode.
Old Tree holds firm. The Searcher sleeps on.

Then, toward evening, the wind and waves relent.
The wind calms down.

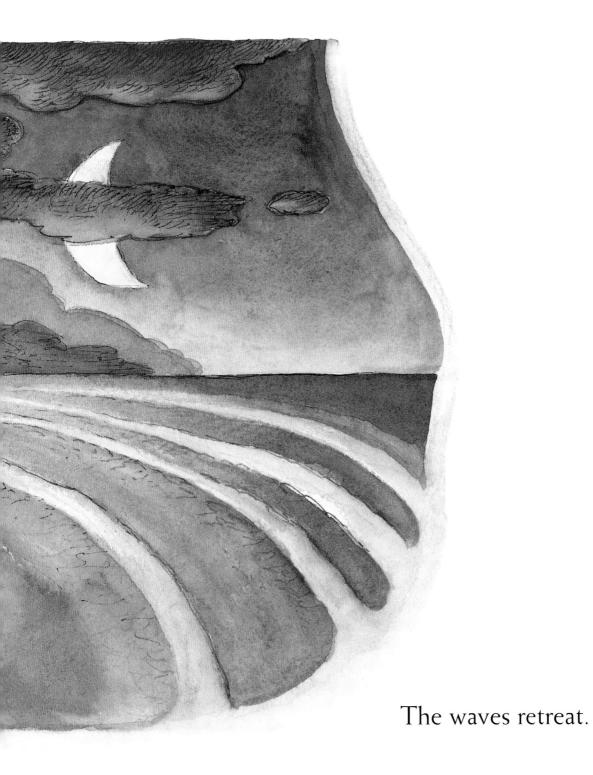

The waves retreat.

The Searcher's stomach rumbles.

He opens his eyes, sits up, and stretches.

He slides down to the ground and heads toward the familiar path.

Suddenly he stops. Something is different.

The grass is wet and covered with leaves.
Broken branches lie scattered about.

The Searcher looks up. Old Tree's branches wave slightly in the breeze. The Searcher watches quietly, then waves back.

Old Tree will be waiting for him when he returns.